This
Treasure Cove Story
belongs to

GUARDIANS OF THE GALAXY

A CENTUM BOOK 978-1-912396-33-7
Published in Great Britain by Centum Books Ltd.
This edition published 2018. 1 3 5 7 9 10 8 6 4 2

© 2018 MARVEL. All rights reserved. marvelHQ.com

Centum Books Ltd, 20 Devon Square, Newton Abbot,
Devon, TQ12 2HR, UK.

www.centumbooksltd.co.uk | books@centumbooksltd.co.uk
CENTUM BOOKS Limited Reg.No. 07641486.

A CIP catalogue record for this book is available
from the British Library.

Printed in China.

centum

MARVEL
GUARDIANS
OF THE GALAXY

By John Sazaklis
Cover illustrated by Patrick Spaziante
Interior illustrated by Michael Borkowski and Michael Atiyeh

Deep in outer space, the **GUARDIANS OF THE GALAXY** are always ready for action! This ragtag team of heroes protects the universe from all sorts of interstellar threats.

Leading the Guardians is Peter Quill, better known as **STAR-LORD**! He is part human and part alien. Star-Lord has amazing strength and speed and his rocket boots blast him into battle!

WHOOSH!

Fighting alongside Star-Lord is the green-skinned **_GAMORA_**. She is the last of her species, an alien race called the Zen-Whoberi. Gamora is a skilled warrior who can heal very quickly from any injury!

ROCKET RACCOON is an expert pilot. He may look cute and fuzzy, but he's no house pet! His sharp claws and enhanced senses make him tough to beat.

His best friend is **GROOT**. He is a tall, tree-like creature who can control plants and grow to an immense size.

This odd couple is a powerful pair!

The last member of the Guardians is the super-strong **DRAX**. He is so tough, he can survive in the extreme cold of space without air, food or water!

The Guardians' home base is called **KNOWHERE**, and **COSMO THE DOG** is their chief of security. Cosmo helps them sniff out trouble!

The Guardians have many different frightful foes throughout the galaxy.

RONAN THE ACCUSER is a sinister soldier with super-speed, super-strength and quick reflexes. He wields a giant hammer called the Universal Weapon. He can use it to crush almost anything!

SMASH!

Like Ronan, **KORATH THE PURSUER** is a member of the alien Kree race. He carries two batons that fire powerful bolts of energy.

The **COLLECTOR** is an ancient being who travels the universe acquiring alien artifacts – especially those with great power!

Unfortunately for the Collector and the fearsome tiger man **TITUS**, Rocket Raccoon and Groot don't play by his rules.

Feared across the galaxy, the space pirate **NEBULA** is a cyborg. She may be part machine, but she's *all* trouble for the Guardians and the bad guys, too!

PROXIMA MIDNIGHT is a master of
hand-to-hand combat. Her deadliest weapon
is a spear made from pure star energy.

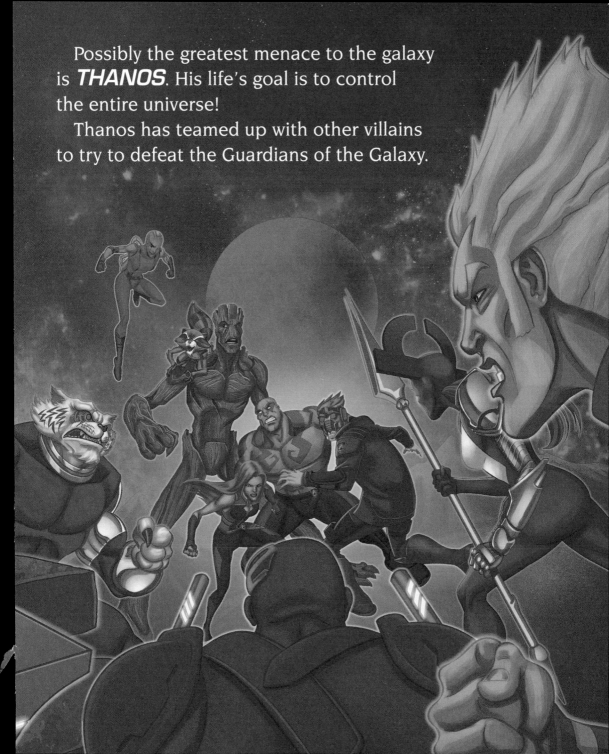

Possibly the greatest menace to the galaxy
is **THANOS**. His life's goal is to control
the entire universe!

Thanos has teamed up with other villains
to try to defeat the Guardians of the Galaxy.

The monstrous **BLACK DWARF**, the energy-blade-wielding **CORVUS GLAIVE** and the mind-eating telepath **SUPERGIANT** are also minions of Thanos.

With all these powerful henchmen at his side, Thanos thinks he is invulnerable… but the Guardians plan to prove him wrong.

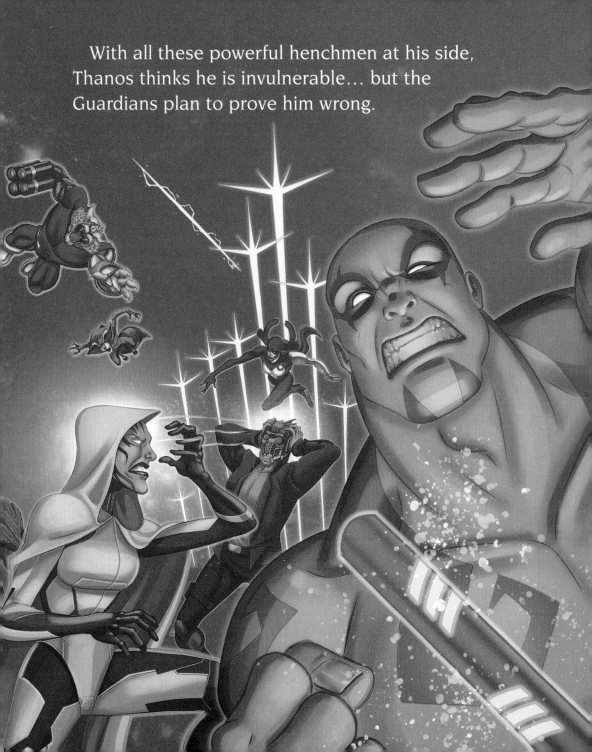

When the Guardians of the Galaxy face off against Thanos and his terrible team, the fight is fierce, but good ultimately overpowers evil.

With the battle won, Star-Lord and his friends head home. The universe will always be safe under the protection of the Guardians of the Galaxy.
GO, GUARDIANS, GO!

Treasure Cove Stories

Book list may be subject to change.

An ongoing series to collect and enjoy!